Marius Brereton

WE'LL MAKE IT

سننجز ذلك

من أجل أحلامهم بالسلام: كادر، صفا، وكل من يحاول تحقيق ذلك.

For their dreams of peace: Kader, Sefâ, and all those who are trying to make it

Marius Brereton

WE'LL MAKE IT

سننجز ذلك

A picture book in two languages (English / Arabic)

Translation: Abdulrahman Abu Rahmah

sefa

كان يا ما كان...

Once upon a time ...

..., not very long ago, there was a small grey elephant called Jubjub, who was carried around on a string.

... ذات مرّة في وقت ليس ببعيد، فيل رمادي صغير يُدعى جُبجُب، الذي كان يُجر على حبل.

»اسمي جُبجُب. جُ-ب-جُ-ب«،
كان يُردّد في حال سأله شخص ما، ولكن
في الغالب لم يقم بذلك أحد.

"My name is Jubjub. J-U-B-J-U-B,"
he would say if anyone asked,
but mostly nobody did.

في أحد الأيام، اضطر جُبجُب مع صديقه إلى القيام برحلة طويلة وشاقة. «لقد سافرنا من قبل» قال جُبجُب، بالإضافة إلى أن الأمور مروّعة هنا.»

One day, Jubjub and his friend had to take a long and difficult journey. "We've been on journeys before," said Jubjub, "and besides, things are terrible here."

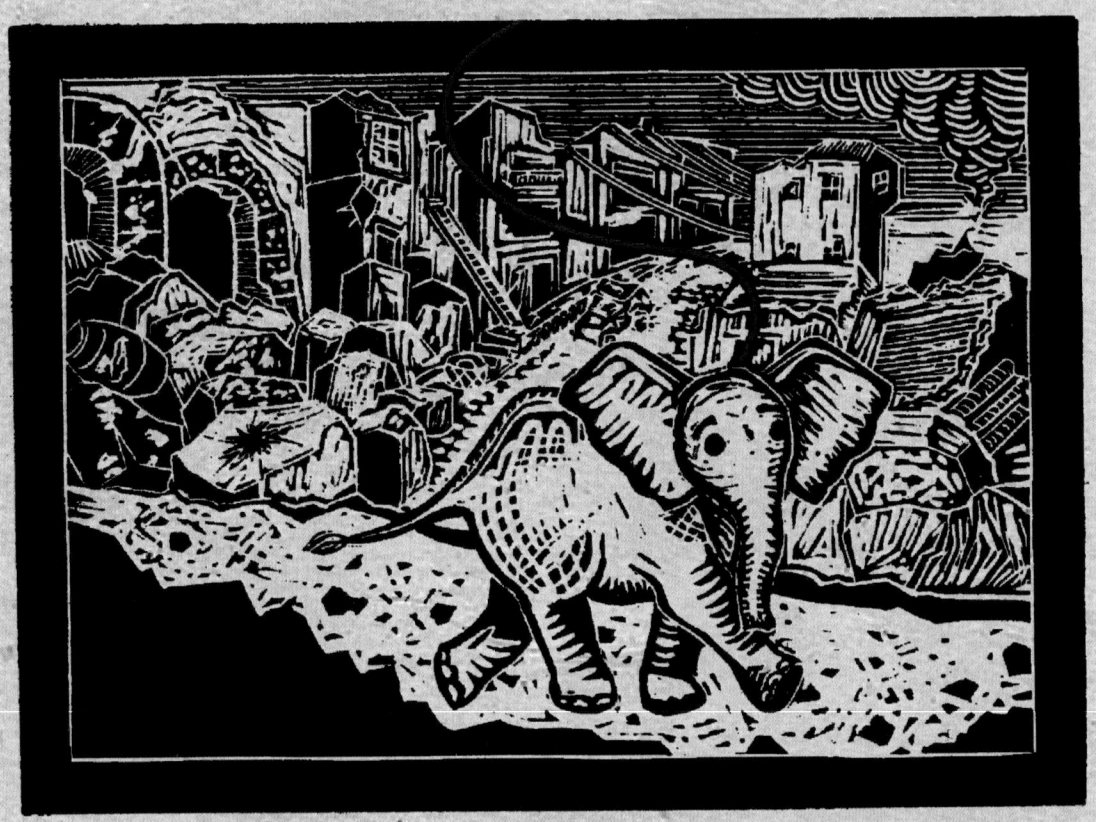

So off they went, down the street, round the corner, and far away. It was quite a bit farther than they had expected.

وهكذا انطلقوا، إلى الشارع، حول المنعطف، مرارًا وتكرارًا، وكانت المسافة أطول مما كانوا يعتقدون.

تعبت أرجلهم من السير، وأقدامهم امتلأت بالتقرّحات.

Their legs were tired of marching and their feet had blisters.

"Oh well," said Jubjub, "we'll make it. Let's wrap our feet in soft leaves. We'll be there soon."

«حسنًا» قال جُبجُب لصديقه، «سننجز ذلك، ربّما سنجد كنزًا.» لذلك بدؤوا بالبحث حولهم ومضوا في طريقهم، خطوة خطوة.

ولكن لا يزال الطريق طويل أمامهم، اضطر جُبجُب وصديقه إلى ركوب الشاحنة مع الغرباء، حيث لسع الرمل عيونهم، على الرغم من أن جُبجُب غطّاهم بأذنيه الكبيرتين.

But it was still a long way. Jubjub and his friend would have to hitch a ride. In the back of the truck, the sand stung their eyes, although Jubjub covered them with his large ears.

There were scary noises and angry faces. There was shouting and pushing. Then someone stole the suitcase with their favorite things.

كانت هناك أصوات مخيفة ووجوه غاضبة، وكذلك أصوات صراخ وأشخاص يتدافعون، وسرق شخص ما حقيبتهم التي كانت تحتوي على أغراضهم المفضّلة.

امتلأت أعين جُبجُب بالدموع، التي سقطت على خدّي الفيل، «ربّما من الأفضل أن نعود» قال جُبجُب، ثمّ قام بالتفكير في جميع الأشياء الفظيعة في المنزل.

Tears welled up in Jubjub's eyes and trickled down his elephant cheeks. "Perhaps it would be better to go back," he said. Then he thought of the terrible things at home.

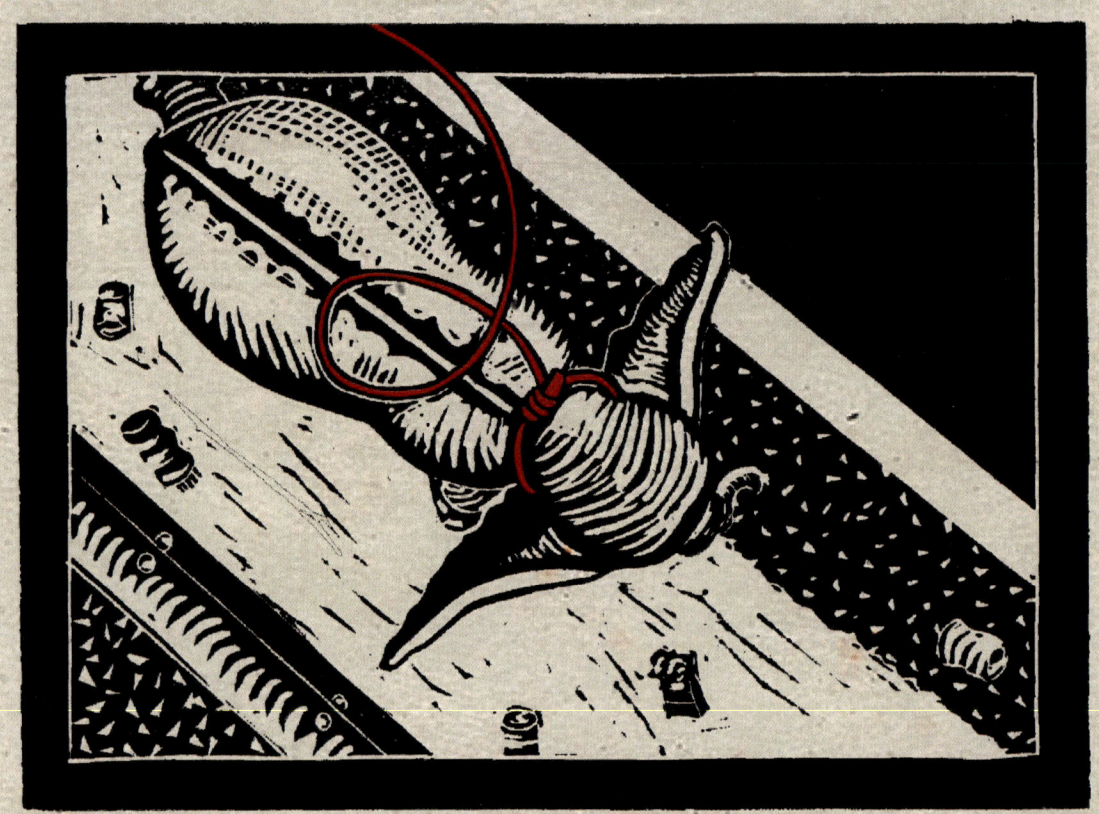

"Oh well," Jubjub said to his friend, "we'll make it. Maybe we'll find treasure." So they looked around and went on a-ways.

They went and they went.

«حسنًا» قال جُبجُب لصديقه، «سننجز ذلك، ربّما سنجد كنزًا.» لذلك بدؤوا بالبحث حولهم ومضوا في طريقهم.

خطوة خطوة.

بعد فترة من الزمن رأوا جزيرة في الأفق، «نستطيع أن نكون قراصنة» صرخ جُبجُب، «لنبحث عن الكنز، يلّا!» وقفزوا على متن القارب.

After a while they saw an island in the distance. "We can be pirates," cried Jubjub, "and find treasure. Yallah!" So they hopped on a boat.

ولكن كانت رحلة القارب وعرة والأمواج عالية، اضطر جُبجُب إلى التمسّك بشدّة بخرطومه، «لا عليك» قال جُبجُب، «سننجز ذلك، فأنا بلا شك متأكّد أنّي أستطيع السباحة جيّدًا.» وبدأ بغناء أغنية صغيرة للفيلة، وكرّر الغناء عدّة مرّات.

But the boat ride was bumpy and the waves were high. Jubjub had to hold on with his trunk.
"Oh well," he said, "we'll make it. I can probably swim really well."
He held on tighter and sang a little elephant song. He sang it a few more times.

عندما وصل جُبجُب وصديقه إلى الشاطئ اندهش الناس، يا ترى كيف أنجزوا ذلك؟ «حسنًا» أجاب جُبجُب، «لم يكن الأمر بهذا السوء، فقد قمت بضخ الماء من على القارب بخرطومي.»

When Jubjub and his friend got to the shore, people were amazed. How had they done it? "Oh well," answered Jubjub, "it wasn't that bad. I squirted water out of the boat with my trunk."

تركوا عوّاماتهم المائية وأطواق النجاة على الشاطئ – لم يكونوا صالحين على أي حال – وانطلقوا مجدّدًا.

They left their water wings and life rings on the beach – they were no good anyway – and off they went.

كانت هناك لافتات على طول الطريق، وعلى الرغم من أن جُبجُب قارئ بارع، إلّا أنه لم يستطيع أن يفهم شيئًا من تلك الحروف ذات الأشكال الغريبة جدًا، «حسنًا» قال جُبجُب، «سننجز ذلك، لنجرّب طريقًا آخر.»

There were signs by the road. Jubjub was a good reader but the letters were odd shapes and he couldn't understand a thing.
"Oh well," he said, "we'll make it. Let's try this way."

وهكذا انطلقوا مجدّدًا، ولكن في الاتجاه الخاطئ، وسد عليهم الطريق سياج مرتفع، فحاول جُبجُب أن يزحف من تحت السياج، ولكن بطنه علقت، والكلاب بدأت بالنباح، وكان جُبجُب يخاف من الكلاب النابحة.

So, off the two of them went. But it was the wrong way and a high fence blocked their path. Jubjub tried to squeeze under the wire but his tummy got stuck. Dogs were barking. Jubjub was scared of barking dogs.

كلاهما سئم من الرحلة، لم تكن مفيدة لا للفيل، ولا لصديقه، ولكن فات الأوان للعودة، إضافة إلى أن الأمور لا تزال كما هي فظيعة في المنزل.

They were both getting tired of the journey. It wasn't good for elephants, nor for elephant friends. But it was too late to go back and, besides, things were still terrible back home.

They would have to try another way. So off they went.

فكان عليهم أن يجدوا طريقًا آخر، وهكذا استمروا بالذهاب.

They went and they went.

خطوة بعد خطوة.

بعد فترة من الزمن رأوا بعضًا من الأشخاص الذين كانوا أيضًا في رحلة، «حسنًا» قال جُبجُب، «لنتبعهم»، فقاموا باتباعهم وسرعان ما وصلوا إلى محطّة قطار.

After a while they saw some people who were also on a journey. "Oh well," said Jubjub, "we'll make it. Let's follow them." So they followed the people and pretty soon they came to a railway station.

"Yippy!" said Jubjub, "We can be train drivers." So, on they hopped. The train was crowded and there were no seats. "Oh well," said Jubjub, "we'll make it. Train drivers never sit down. Yallah!" Off they choofed.

«رائع!» قال جُبجُب، نستطيع أن نلعب دور سائقي القطار»، وصعدوا على متن القطار المزدحم ولكن لم تكن هناك مقاعد خالية، «حسنًا» أجاب جُبجُب، «سننجز ذلك، سائقي القطار لا يجلسون أبدًا، يلّا!» وانطلقوا.

خطوة بعد خطوة. They choofed and they choofed.

After a while, Jubjub and his friend got really tired. It was hard to find a comfy place to sleep, so Jubjub rolled up his trunk for a pillow.

بعد فترة من الزمن، أصاب جُبجُب وصديقه بالتعب الشديد، وكان من الصعب العثور على مكان مريح للنوم، فلف جُبجُب خرطومه على شكل وسادة.

أخيرًا، وصل القطار إلى المحطّة، وفي الوقت المناسب حيث سئموا من لعب دور سائق القطار. كان الناس ينتظرون على المنصّة ويوزّعون أشياءًا رائعة، مدّ جُبجُب خرطومه وأخذ بعضًا من الحلوى وقنينة ماء ليشاركها مع صديقه.

Finally, the train pulled into a station. Anyway, they were tired of being train drivers. People were waiting on the platform and handing out nice things. Jubjub reached out with his trunk and took some sweets and a bottle of water to share.

»ألم أقل لك« قال جُبجُب، »ها نحن هنا، لقد أنجزنا ذلك بالفعل.«

"See," said Jubjub, "we're here. We really made it."

ACKNOWLEDGEMENTS • شكر وتقدير

Wiki, Jan, Janusz, Clara, Anka, Iris, Akil, Aras, Dora, Valentine, Annika, Jota, Sara, U, Ki, Rose, and Toby

More bilingual books from Sefa

Tim can't fall asleep. His little wolf is missing! Perhaps he forgot him outside? Tim heads out all alone into the night – and unexpectedly encounters some friends ...

For children from 2 years. With online audiobook and video in English.

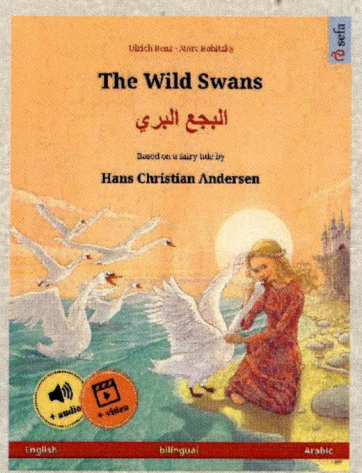

"The Wild Swans" by Hans Christian Andersen is, with good reason, one of the world's most popular fairy tales. In its timeless form it addresses the issues out of which human dramas are made: fear, bravery, love, betrayal, separation and reunion.
The edition at hand is a lovingly illustrated picture book recounting Andersen's fairy tale in a sensitive and child-friendly form.

For children from 5 years. With online audiobook and video in English.

Lulu can't fall asleep. All her cuddly toys are dreaming already – the shark, the elephant, the little mouse, the dragon, the kangaroo, and the lion cub. Even the bear has trouble keeping his eyes open ...

Hey bear, will you take me along into your dream?

Thus begins a journey for Lulu that leads her through the dreams of her cuddly toys – and finally to her own most beautiful dream.

For children from 5 years. With online audiobook and video in English.

© 2022 Sefa Verlag Kirsten Bödeker, Lübeck, Germany

All rights reserved
Linocuts and text:
Marius Brereton Cover art: Annika Roux using a linocut by Marius Brereton
Layout: Annika Roux, Juan Pablo Vega Campos

ISBN 9783756310036
www.sefa-verlag.de

Made in the USA
Monee, IL
26 December 2024